This Bing book belongs to:

. . . .

Copyright © 2019 Acamar Films Ltd

First published in Great Britain in 2016 by HarperCollins *Children's Books*,
a division of HarperCollins *Publishers* Ltd, 1 London Bridge Street, London SE1 9GF

1 3 5 7 9 10 8 6 4 2

ISBN: 978-0-00-797948-6

The Bing television series is an Acamar Films production, co-produced in association with Brown Bag Films,
and adapted from the original books by Ted Dewan

Based on the script 'Giving' by Lead Writer Gillian Corderoy and Team Writers Lucy Murphy, Mikael Shields and An Vrombaut

Edited by Stella Gurney, Freddie Hutchins and An Vrombaut

Designed by Gary Knight

Printed in China

Birthday Present

HarperCollins *Children's Books*

Round the corner, not far away,
Bing is choosing a present today.

Bing spots something.
"Whoa – look Flop! I'm going to get Sula this!
It has a tippy bit, big wheels and it goes,

brrrrm!
Brrrrrm!

"Oh…" says Flop.
"Is a monster truck
something that Sula
would like, Bing?"

"Yup!"

"Let's think – what sort of things does Sula like, Bing?"

"Umm, she likes her **fairy wings... and dancing...** and her magic wand!"

"And does she like **cars?**" asks Flop. "Umm, **no,**" giggles Bing. "Sula likes **sparkly, shiny, pink** things."

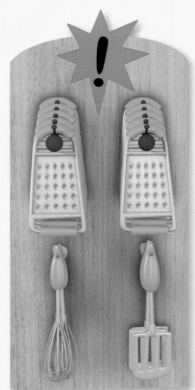

Bing sees something on the wall. "Ooh, **that's** shiny!"

"It is," agrees Flop. "But is it a **Sula** thing?"

"**No**," laughs Bing. "It's not a Sula thing."

Flop finds a rubber duck.

"What about this, Bing?"

"Silly Flop!" giggles Bing.
"It's not **bath** time, it's **birthday** time!"

Then Padget has an idea.

"Bing – how about this special,
spinny wand?"

Oh! Bing takes the wand from Padget.
He presses the button.

"It's **sparkly!**" says Bing. "I **love** it!"

"Oh, **Bing** – that's **definitely** a Sula thing," says Flop. "Shall we get it for her?"

"Ye-ess," says Bing, staring at the wand. "It's all...

spinny."

Padget puts
the wand in a
special bag.

"Can I carry it,
Flop?" asks Bing.

"Sure. Sula's
going to love
her present, Bing.
Shall we go and
give it to her?"

"Um… yup."

Outside, Bing asks if he can have
another look at the spinny wand.
"Not in the middle of the road, Bing.
Let's wait until we get into the park."

In the park, Bing takes the wand back out of the bag.

"Oh... I love this spinny wand, Flop... Maybe... we can give Sula her present tomorrow?"

"Well," says Flop. "We could Bing, but it's Sula's birthday today. And she's looking forward to seeing you."

"Oh... yes," says Bing.

Bing and Flop arrive at Sula's house.
"Don't you want to ring the bell, Bing?" asks Flop.

"Umm...OK," says Bing.

Ding-dong!

Phoooooo!

"Hi Bing, it's me!" shouts Sula. "Come inside! It's my birthday!"

Amma is waiting upstairs.

"Hello, Bing – hello, Flop! Oh, do I see something for the birthday girl?"

"Ooh!" squeals Sula. "It's for ME! It's my present!"

"Yes," says Flop. "Bing chose something especially for YOU, Sula!"

Bing takes a deep breath. He gives the bag to Sula. "Happy Birthday, Sula."

"**Aaah!** Thank you, Bing – it's a wand!" says Sula, waving it about. "Oh, it's so **spinny! I love** it!"

"Oh Sula, look what that clever bunny bought you," smiles Amma.

Bing watches Sula.
"I love the spinny wand too, Flop. I... wanted it."

"Yes, I can see that, Bing," says Flop.
"But look at Sula. Your present has
made her **really happy.**"

"This is my **best best best best best** present!" says Sula, dancing over to Bing.

Then she notices another button on the wand.

"It does music!"

"Flop," cries Bing.
"I didn't know it did
music!"

Everyone
dances
to the spinny wand.

"I **love** my spinny wand," says Sula.

"I **choosed** it for you, Sula," says Bing proudly.

"For your **birthday!**"

"Thank you, Bing!"

Sula gives Bing a **big** kiss.

Good for you, Bing Bunny!

Hi! It was Sula's birthday, so I choosed her a really **really** good birthday present.

It was a **sparkly, spinny** wand!

And I wanted to keep it.

But I had to give it to Sula.
And that was hard.

But Sula loved it!
And she found a music
button which made it
even better!

Sometimes it's hard to give a
present away. But if you give
it to a friend, you can play
with it together!

Giving a present...

it's a **Bing** thing.